P9-ECU-419

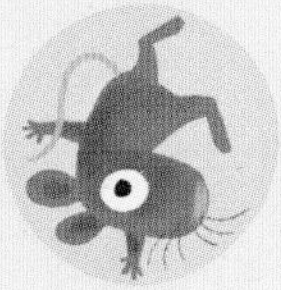

Also look for:

BOBO AND PUP-PUP: LET'S MAKE CAKE!

BOBO and PUP-PUP

WE LOVE BUBBLES!

by Vikram Madan

illustrated by Nicola Slater

A STEPPING STONE BOOK™

Random House   New York

For Madhu, who believes in me, more than anyone
—V.M.

To Leo and Finn
—N.S.

Text copyright © 2021 by Vikram Madan
Cover art and interior illustrations copyright © 2021 by Nicola Slater

All rights reserved. Published in the United States by Random House Children's Books,
a division of Penguin Random House LLC, New York.

Random House and the colophon are registered trademarks and A Stepping Stone Book
and the colophon are trademarks of Penguin Random House LLC.

Visit us on the Web!
rhcbooks.com

Educators and librarians, for a variety of teaching tools, visit us at RHTeachersLibrarians.com

Library of Congress Cataloging-in-Publication Data
Names: Madan, Vikram, author. | Slater, Nicola, illustrator.
Title: We love bubbles! / by Vikram Madan ; illustrated by Nicola Slater.
Description: First edition. | New York : Random House Children's Books, [2021] |
Series: A stepping stone book | Audience: Ages 4–7. | Audience: Grades K–1. |
Summary: Pup-Pup loves blowing bubbles and does not like having best friend Bobo pop
all of them, but when Pup-Pup uses super-strong bubble mix, bubble trouble ensues.
Identifiers: LCCN 2019050352 (print) | LCCN 2019050353 (ebook) | ISBN 978-0-593-12065-1
(hardcover) | ISBN 978-0-593-12066-8 (library binding) | ISBN 978-0-593-12067-5 (ebook)
Subjects: CYAC: Bubbles—Fiction. | Friendship—Fiction. | Monkeys—Fiction. | Dogs—Fiction.
Classification: LCC PZ7.1.M2589 We 2021 (print) | LCC PZ7.1.M2589 (ebook) | DDC [E]—dc23

MANUFACTURED IN CHINA
10 9 8 7 6 5 4 3 2 1
First Edition

Contents

Chapter 1
Bubbles!

bubble soap mix

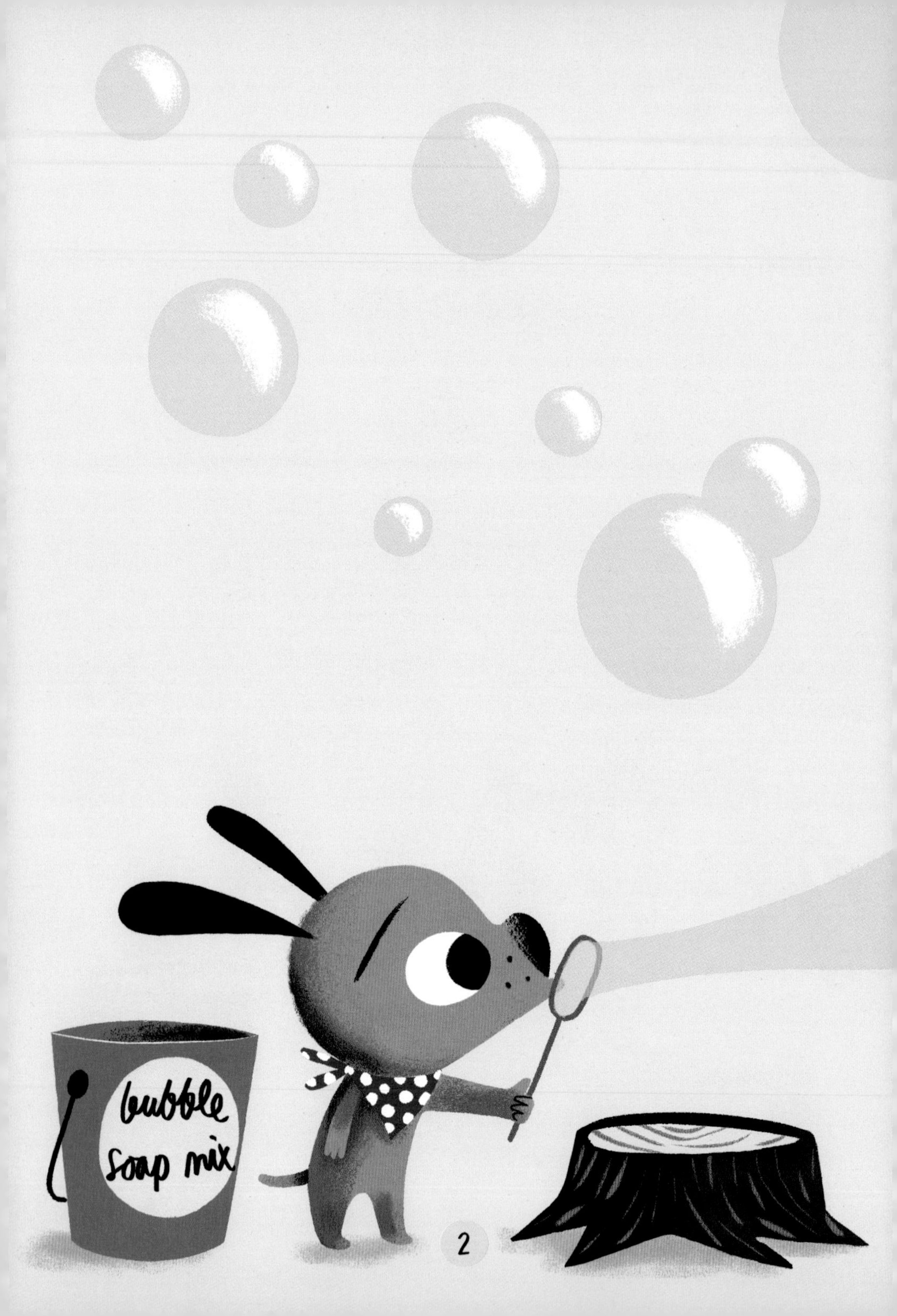
bubble
soap mix

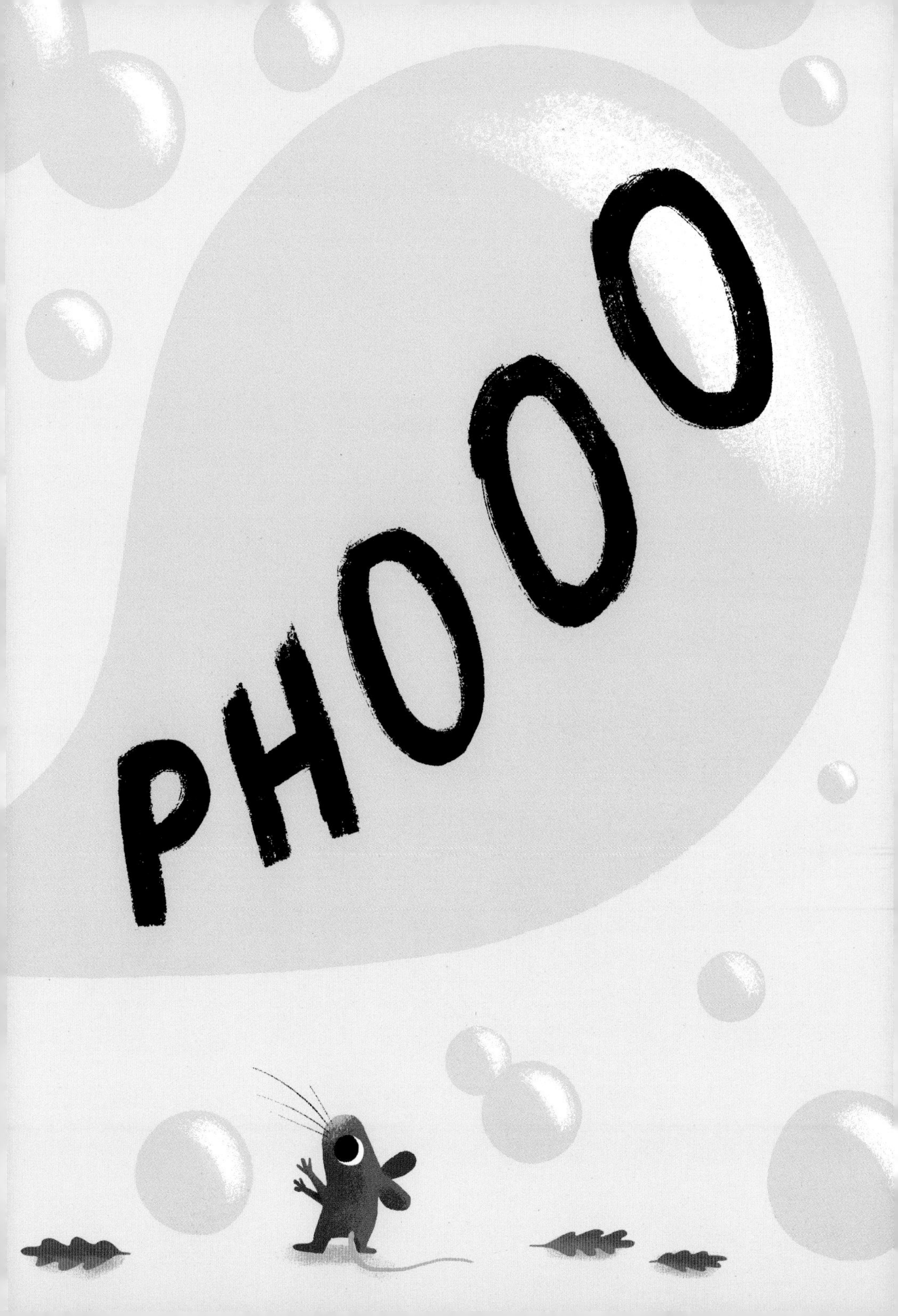
PHOOO

I LOVE bubbles!!!

bubble soap mix

4

BUBBLES?
I LOVE bubbles, too!!!

5

I love BLOWING bubbles!!!

bubble soap mix

6

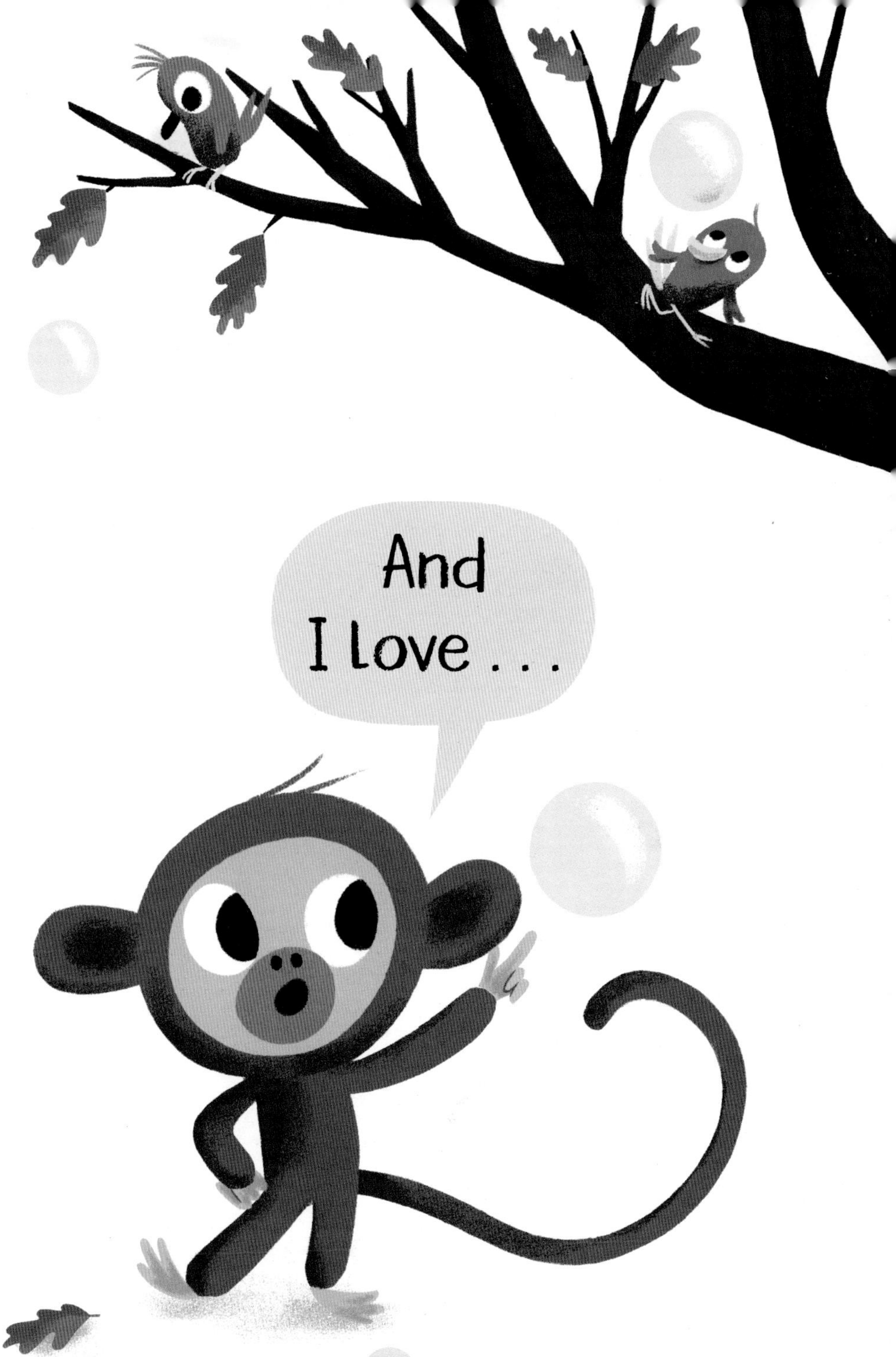
And
I love . . .

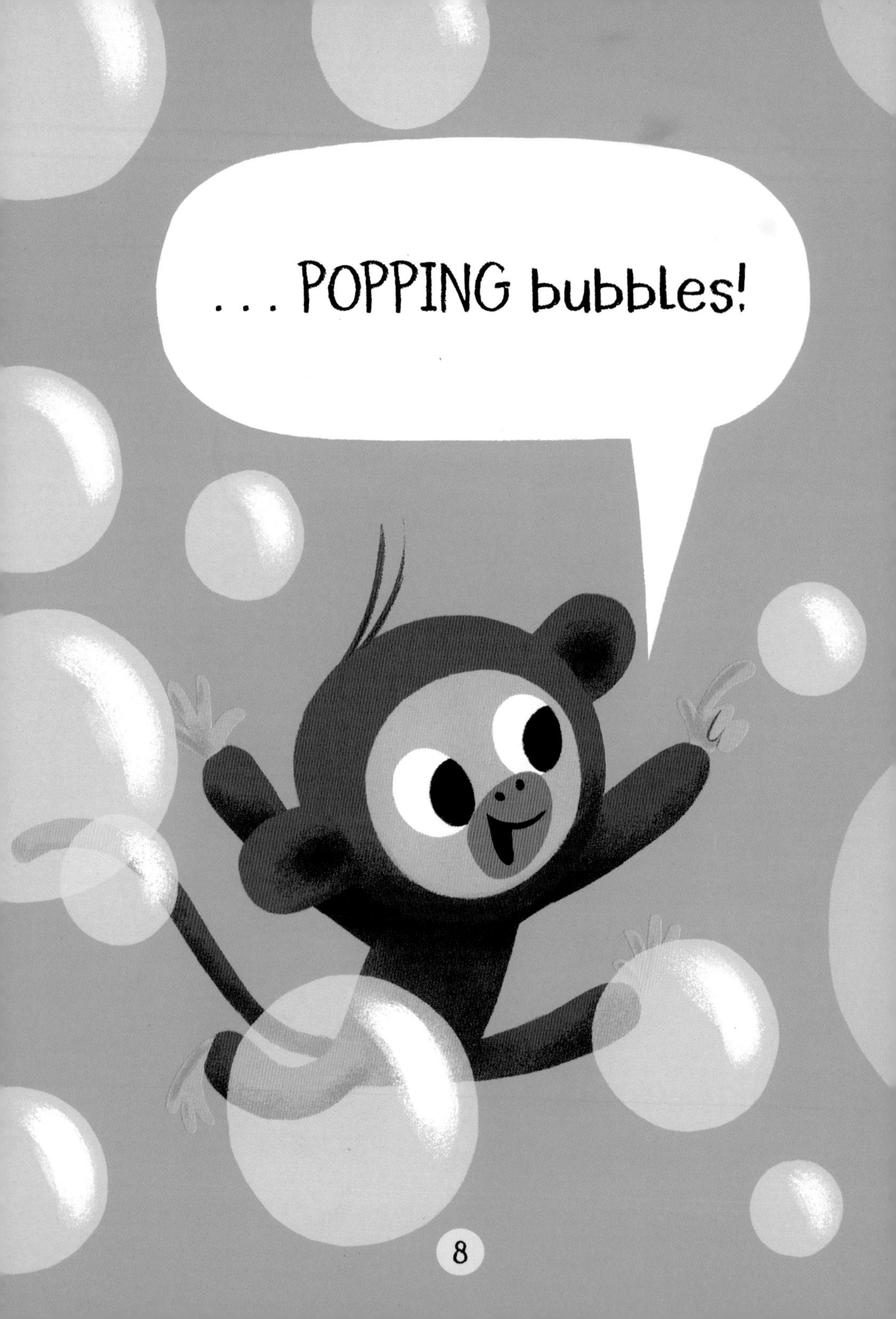
. . . POPPING bubbles!

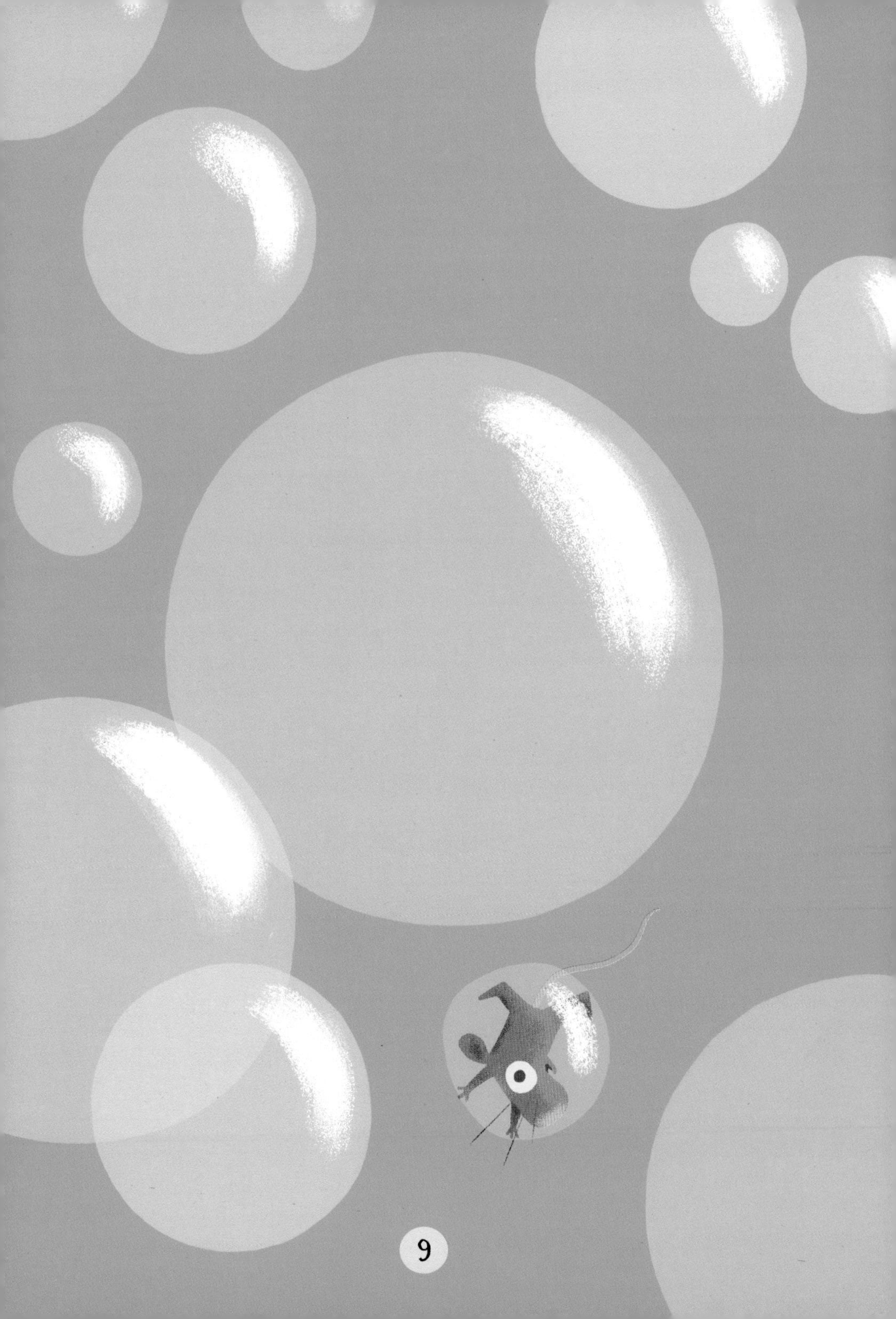

POP!

POP!

POP!

POP!

POP!

POP!

POP!

Bobo! You popped all my bubbles!

Yes, I popped ALL your bubbles! High five!

bubble soap mix

Chapter 2
MORE Bubbles!

Popping bubbles is SO MUCH FUN!

12

POP

I LOVE POPPING BUBBLES!

bubl
soap

14

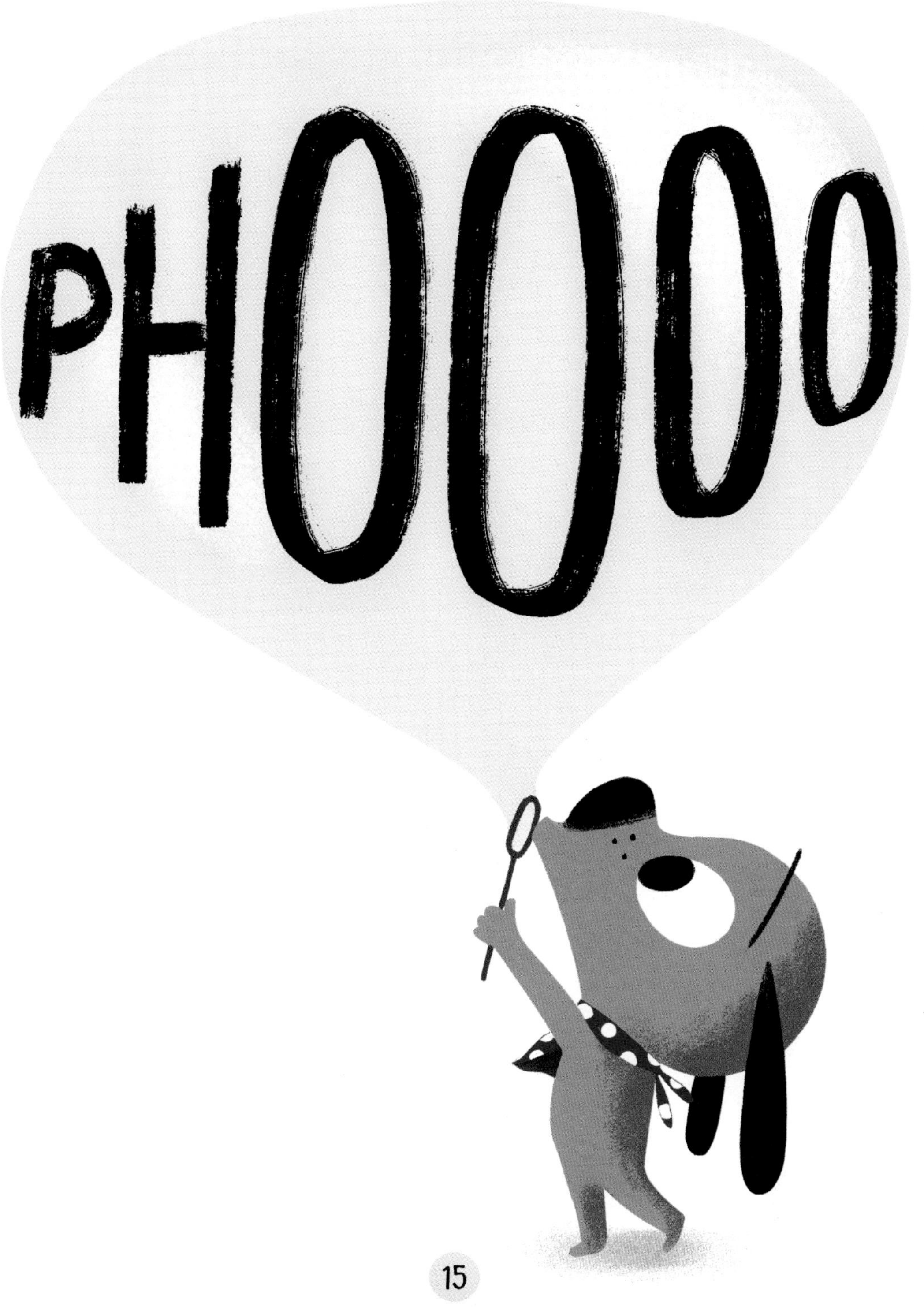
PHOOOO

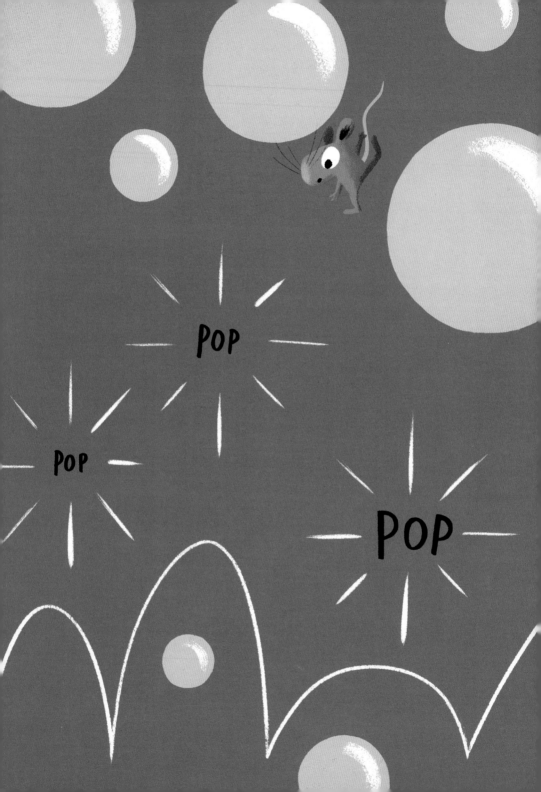

POP

POP

POP

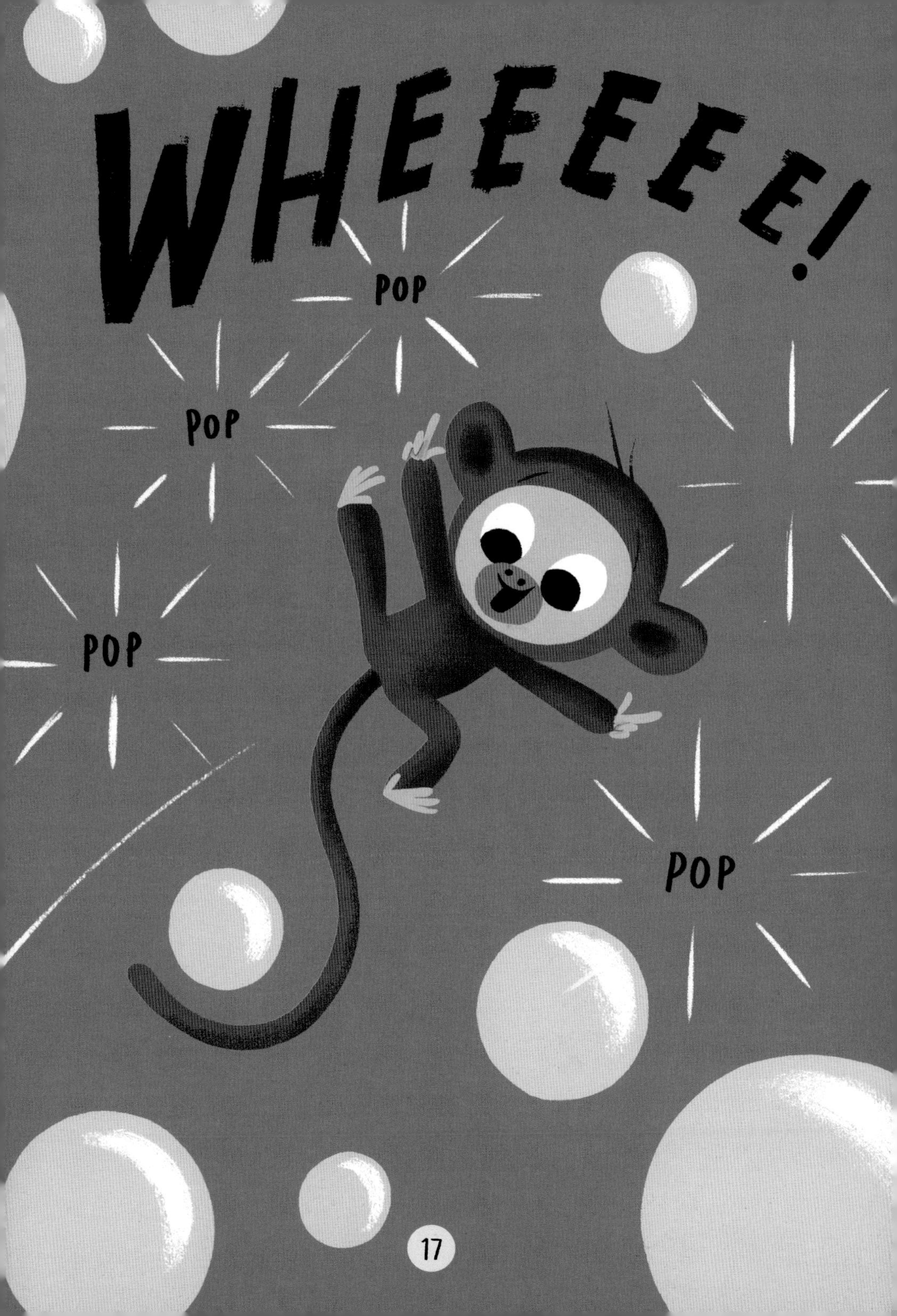
WHEEEEEE!
POP
POP
POP
POP

I'm just going to keep blowing bubbles. . . .

I'm just
going to
keep
popping
bubbles. . . .

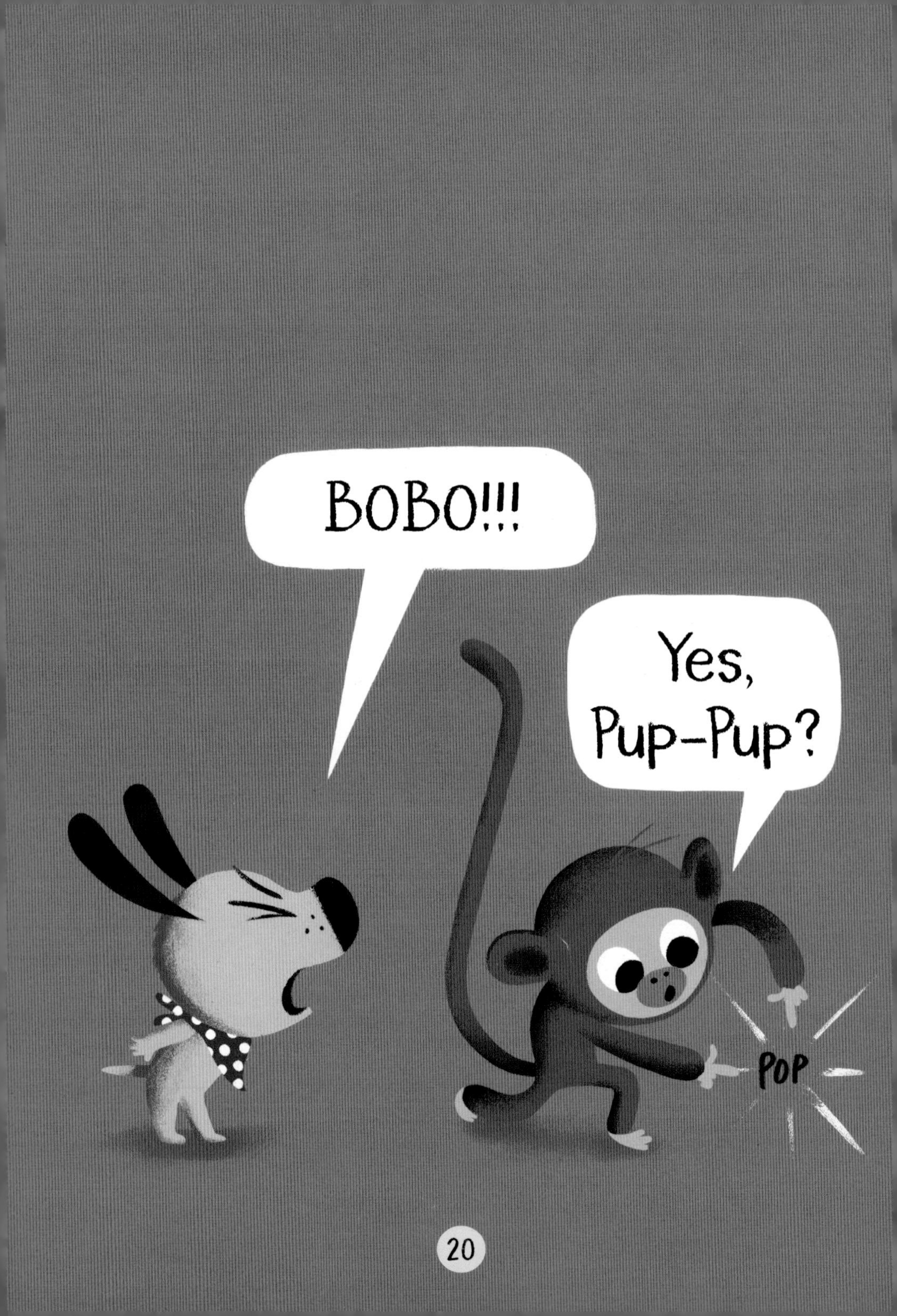
BOBO!!!
Yes, Pup-Pup?
POP

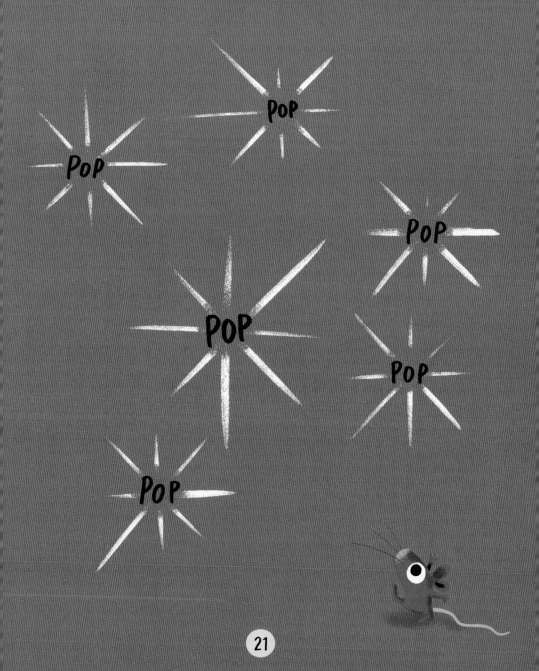

POP

POP

POP

POP

POP

POP

POP

STOP POPPING MY BUBBLES!!!

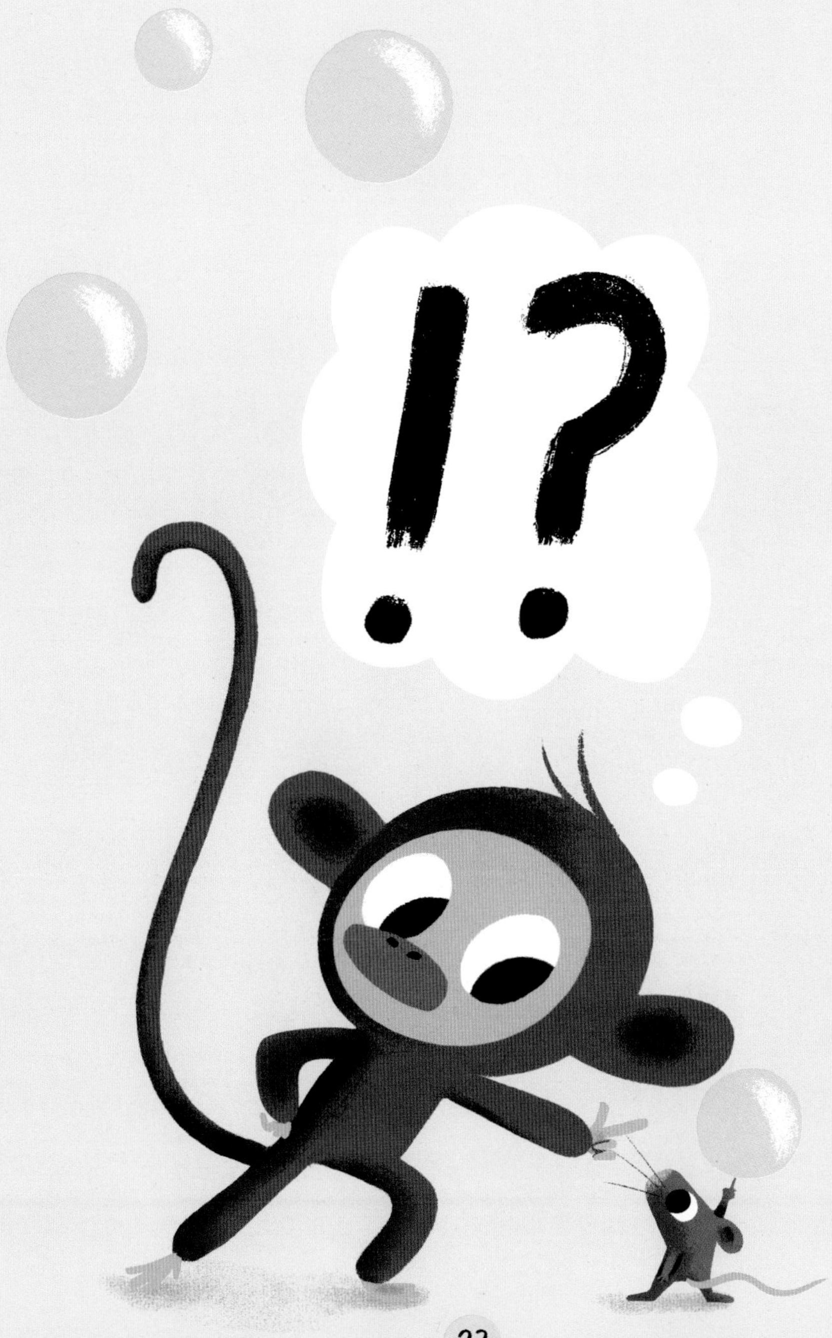
!?

I can't help it.
When I see a bubble,
I just have to POP it!

Chapter 3
Better Bubbles?

Hey, what's that?

hee hee hee

SUPER
BUBBLE
MIX

26

Super bubble mix, for making super-strong bubbles.

SUPER BUBBLE MIX

27

HUMPH!

The bubbles will be so strong . . .

. . . NO ONE can POP them!

29

I LOVE
blowing
bubbles!

PHOOOO

30

I LOVE popping bubbles!

hee hee hee

31

Chapter 4
Bubble Trouble!

SUPER BUBBLE MIX

PHOOOO

POKE POKE

Huh?
It's not
popping!

33

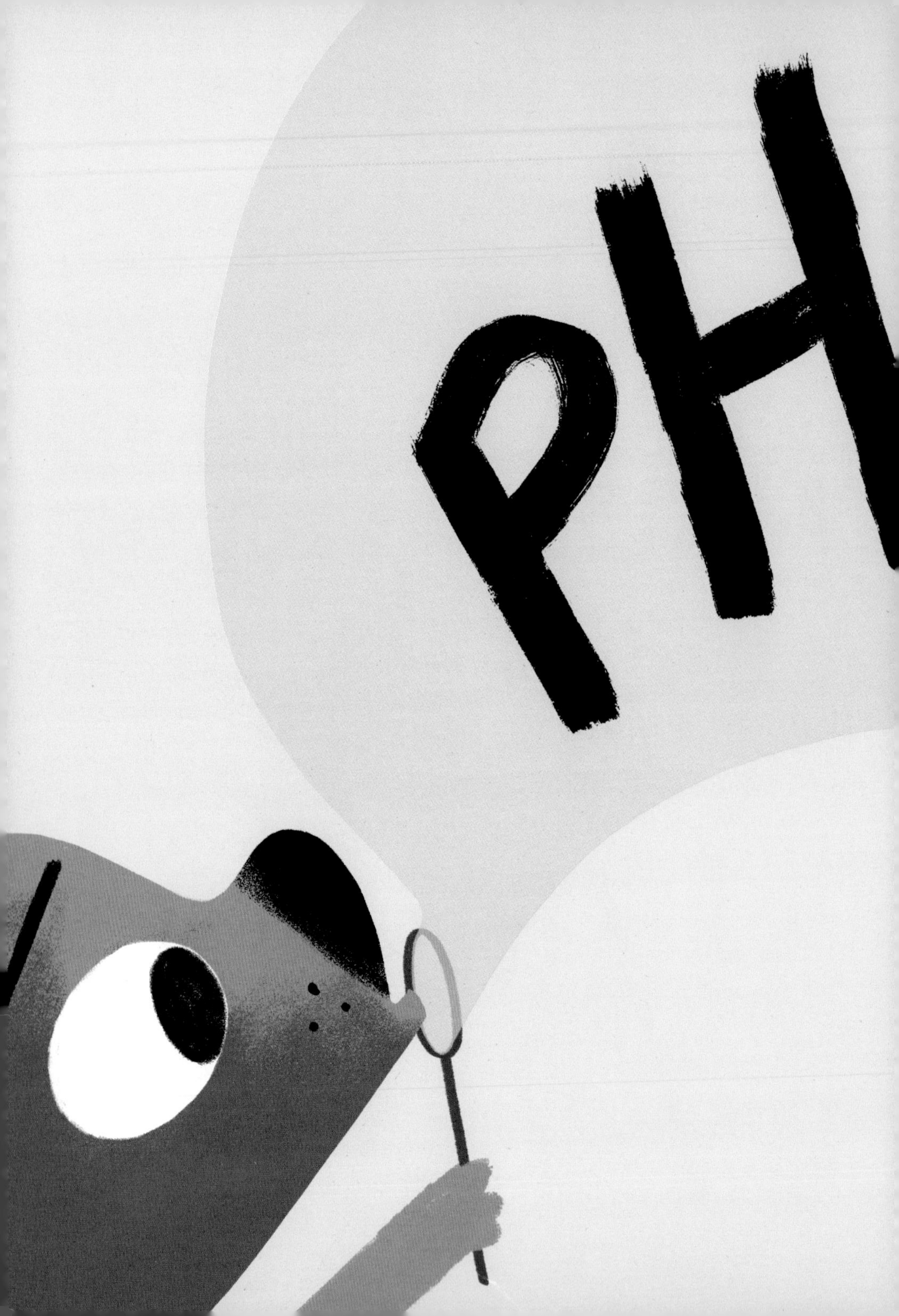
PH

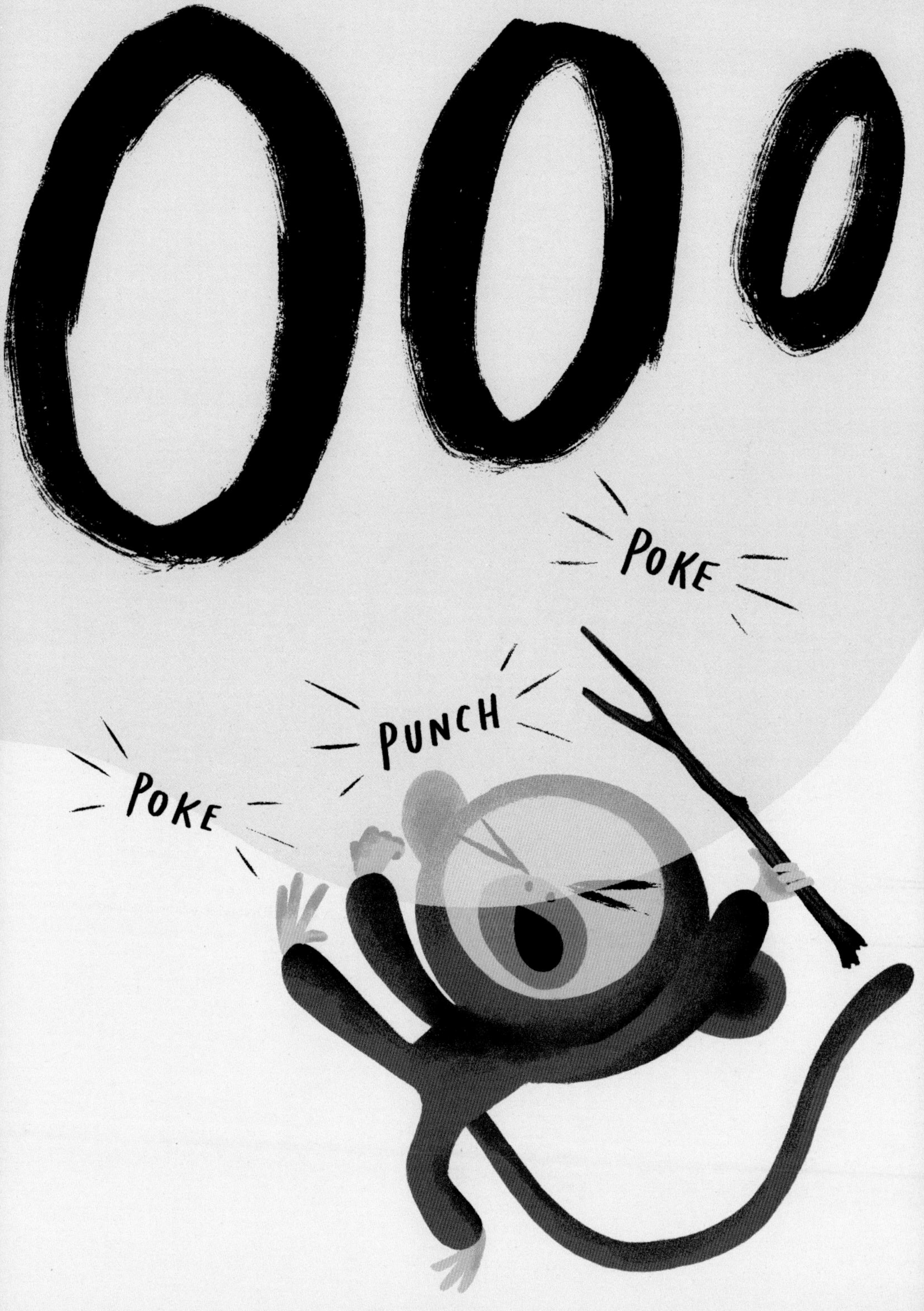
OOo
POKE
PUNCH
POKE

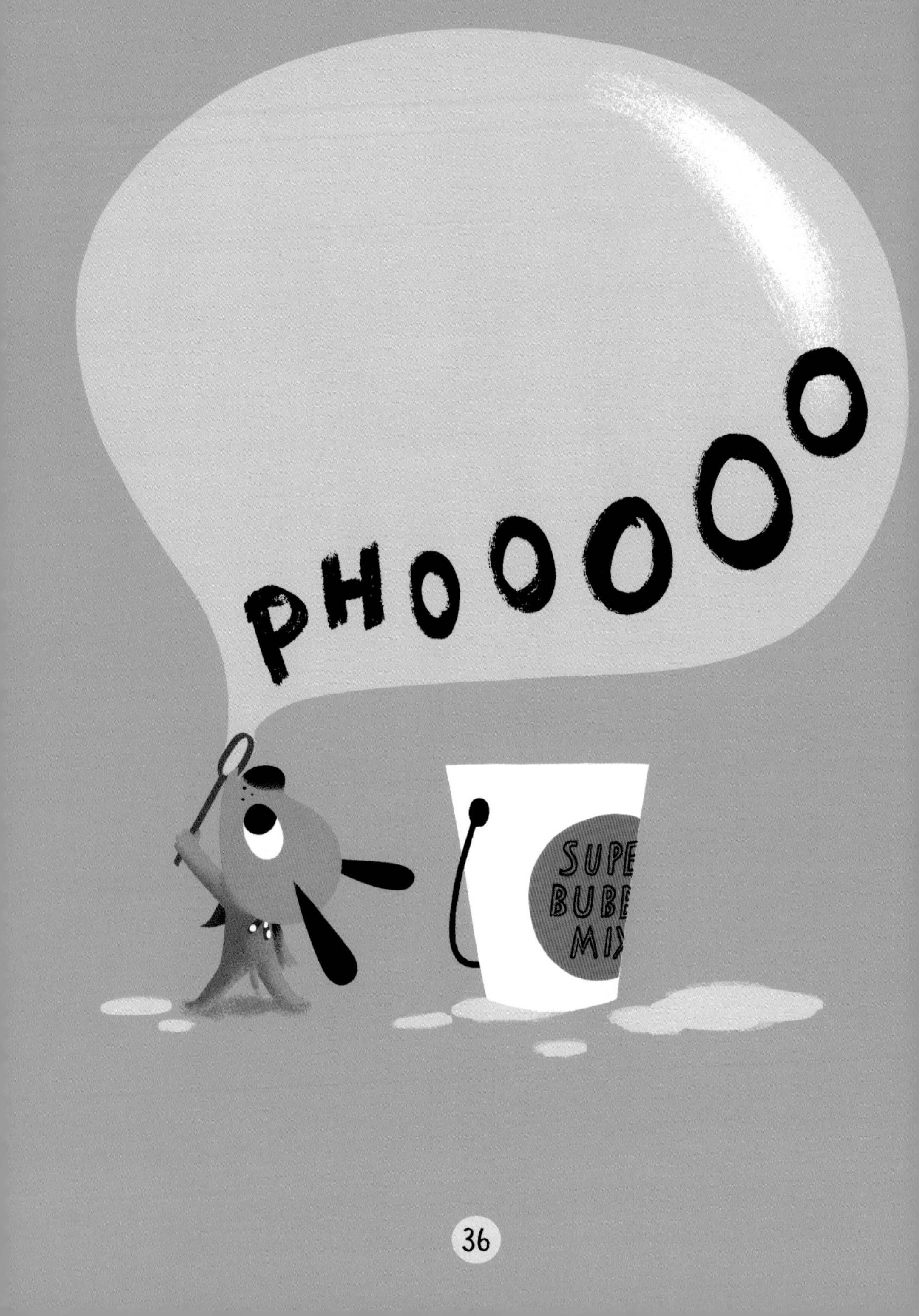
PHOOOOO
SUPE
BUBB
MIX

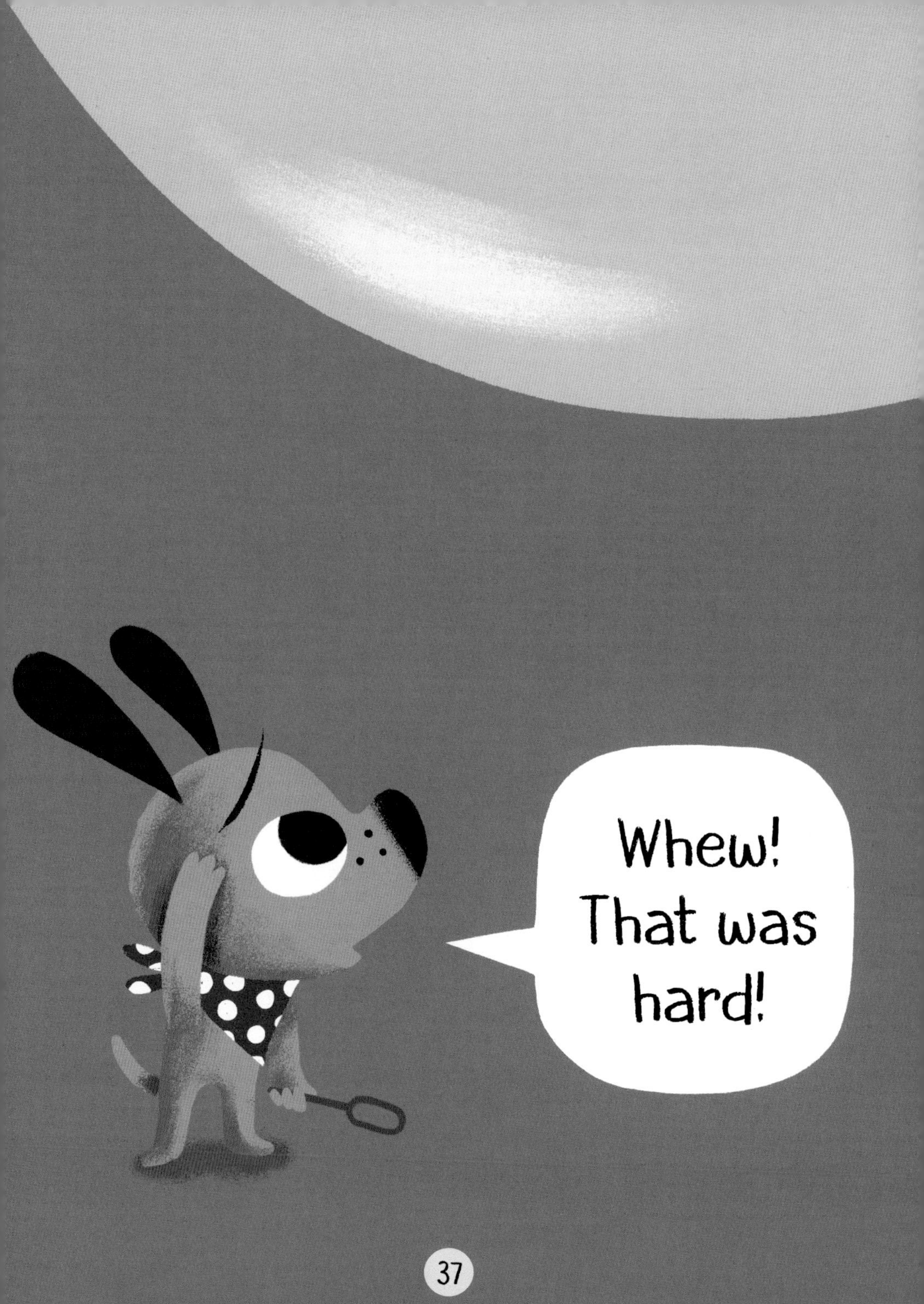
Whew! That was hard!

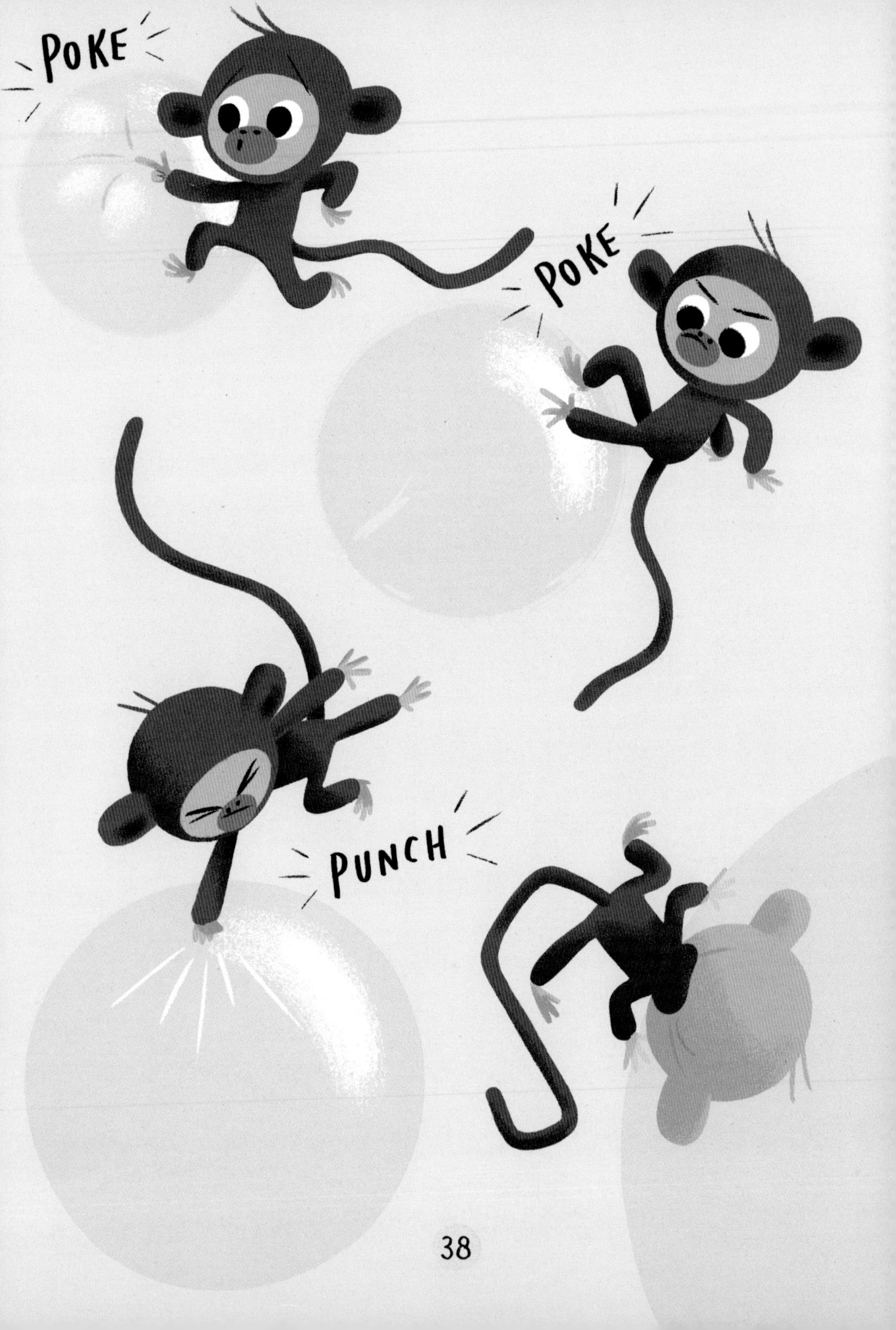
POKE
POKE
PUNCH

Yikes!

SQUEAK!

SQUISH! BLOOP!

Gulp!

Go ahead! Try popping THAT bubble!

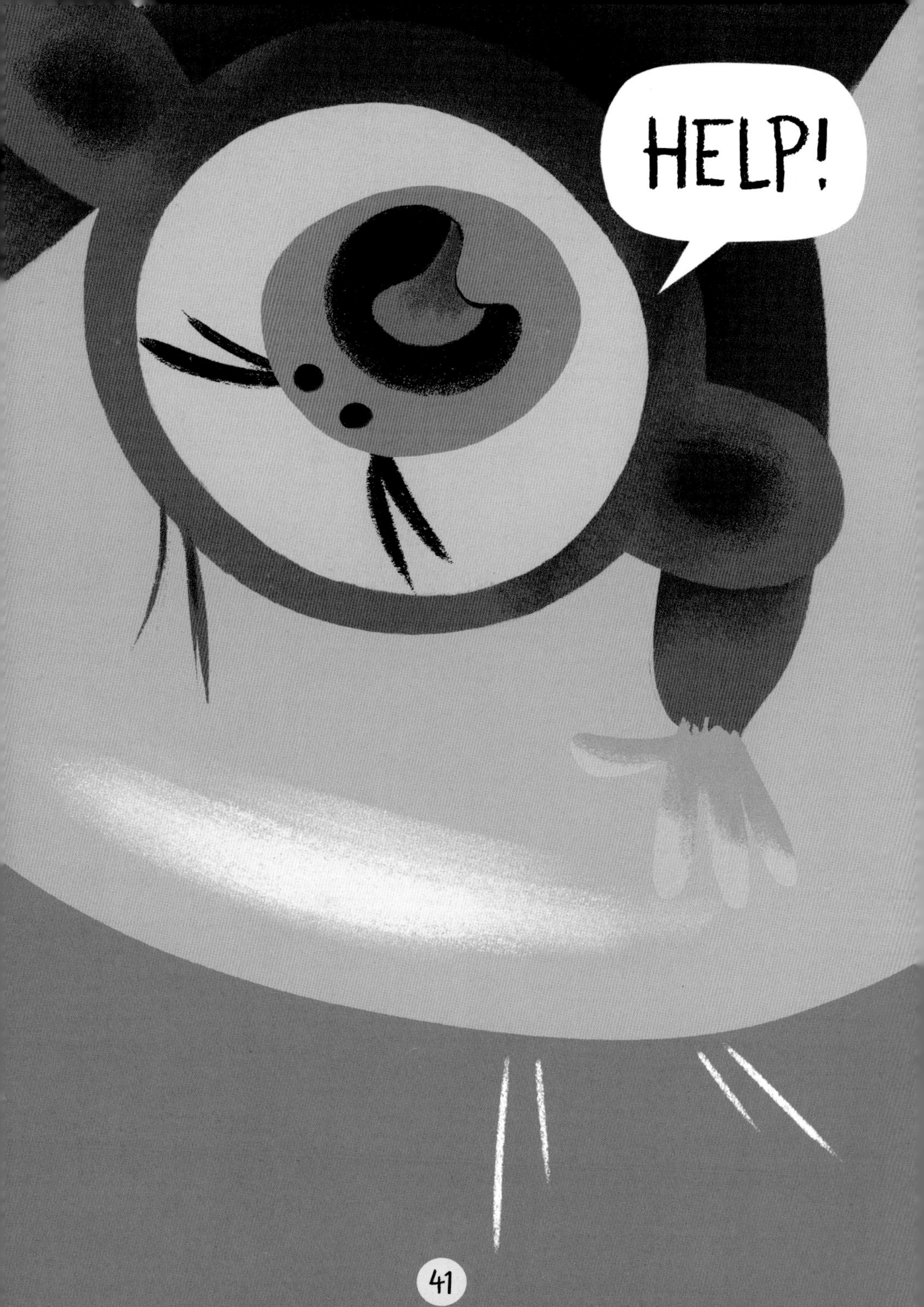
HELP!

Bobo?

Bobo!!

SUPER
BUBBLE
MIX

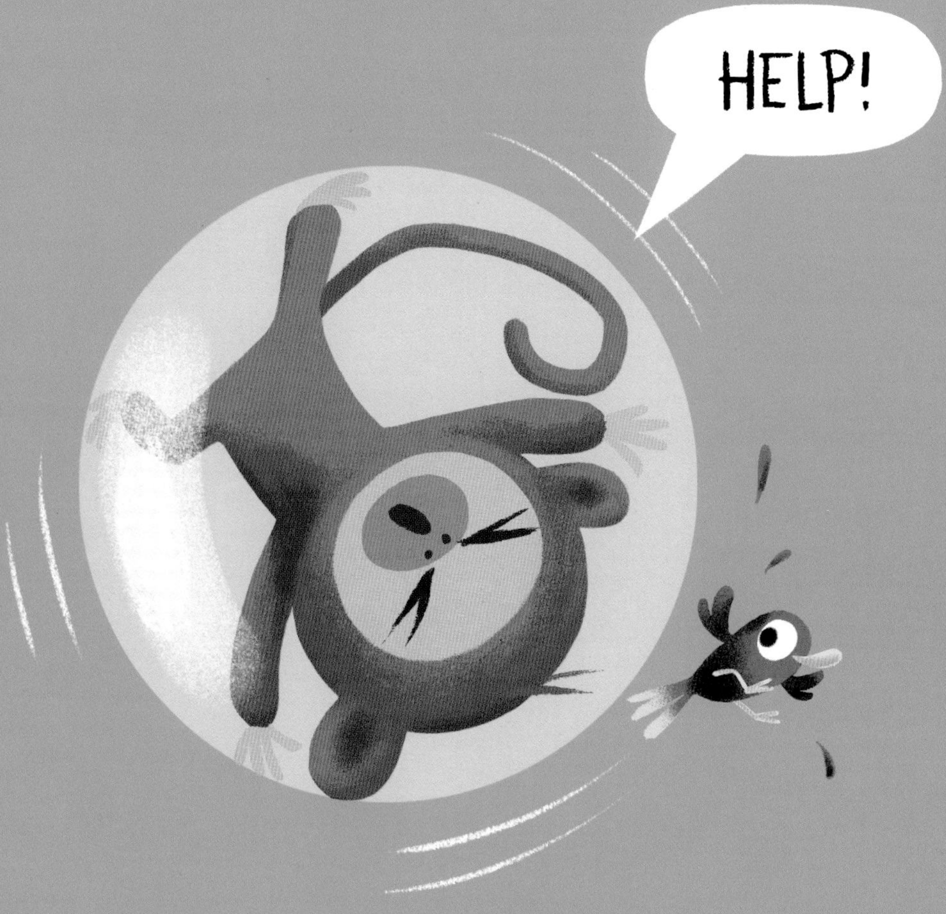
HELP!

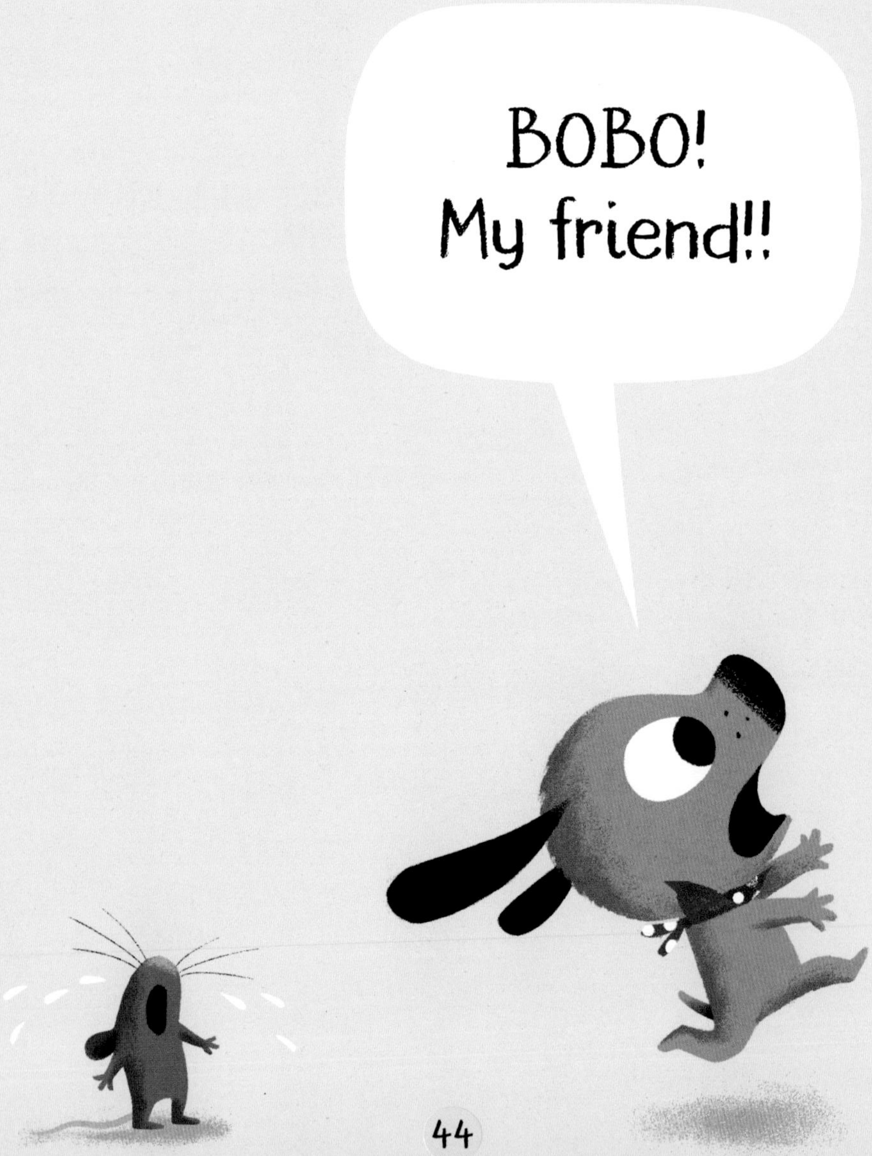
BOBO!
My friend!!

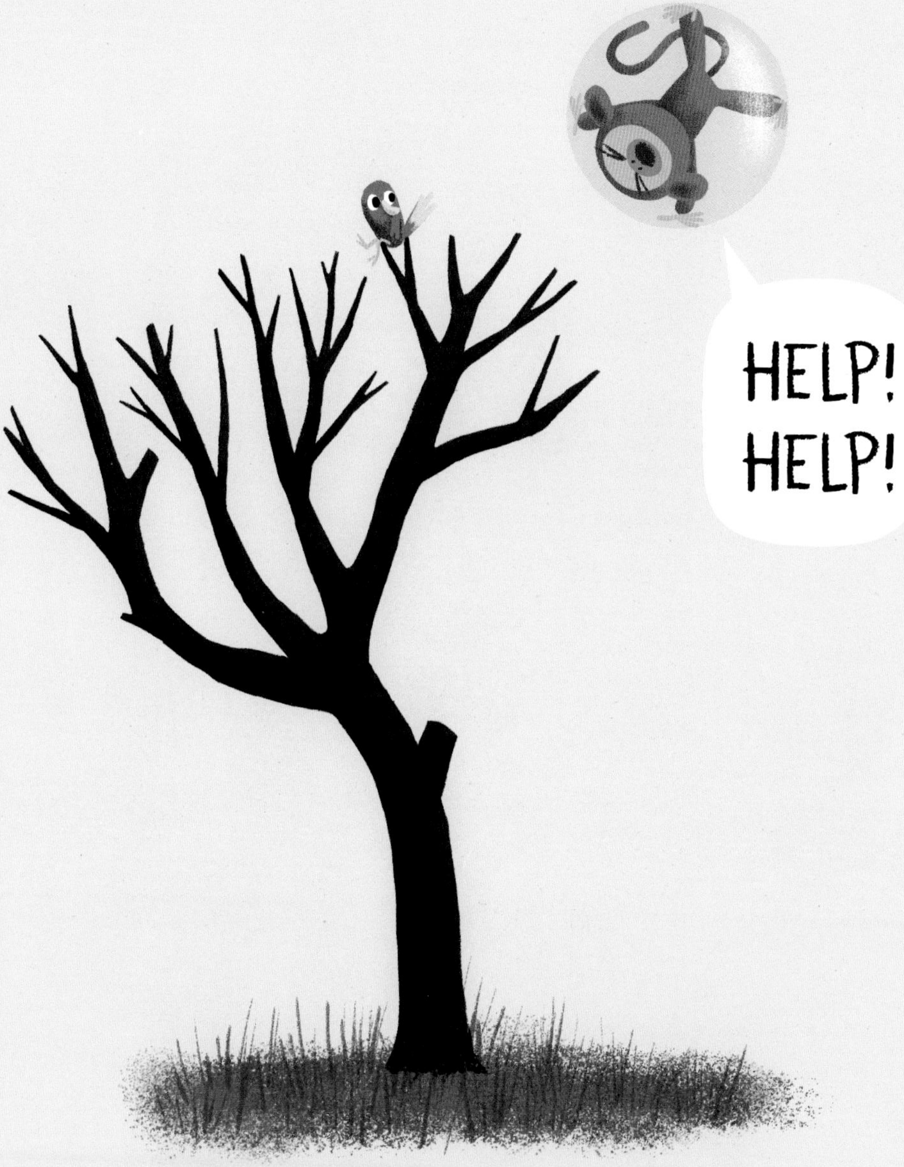
HELP!
HELP!

I will save you, Bobo!

SPROING!

Save me,
Pup-Pup!
Save me!

This bubble is TOO strong!

pound pound pound

Pup-Pup, save yourself!

Wait, I have an idea!

CHOMP!

49

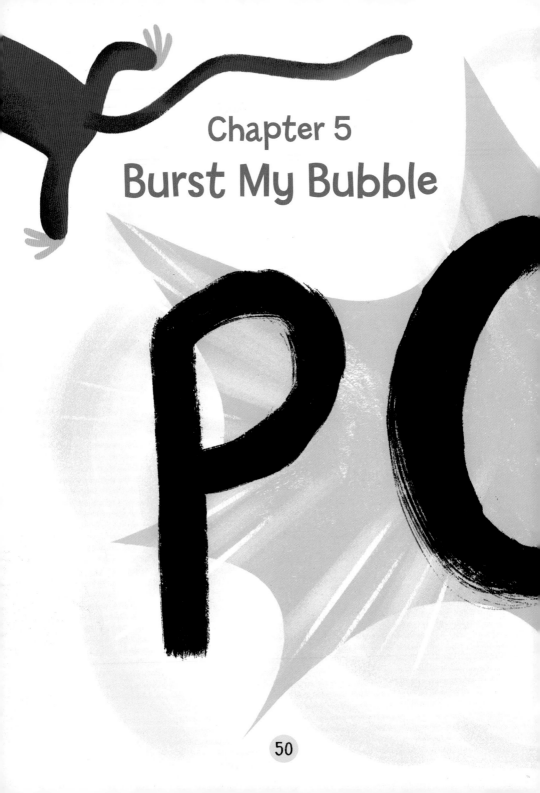

Chapter 5
Burst My Bubble

50

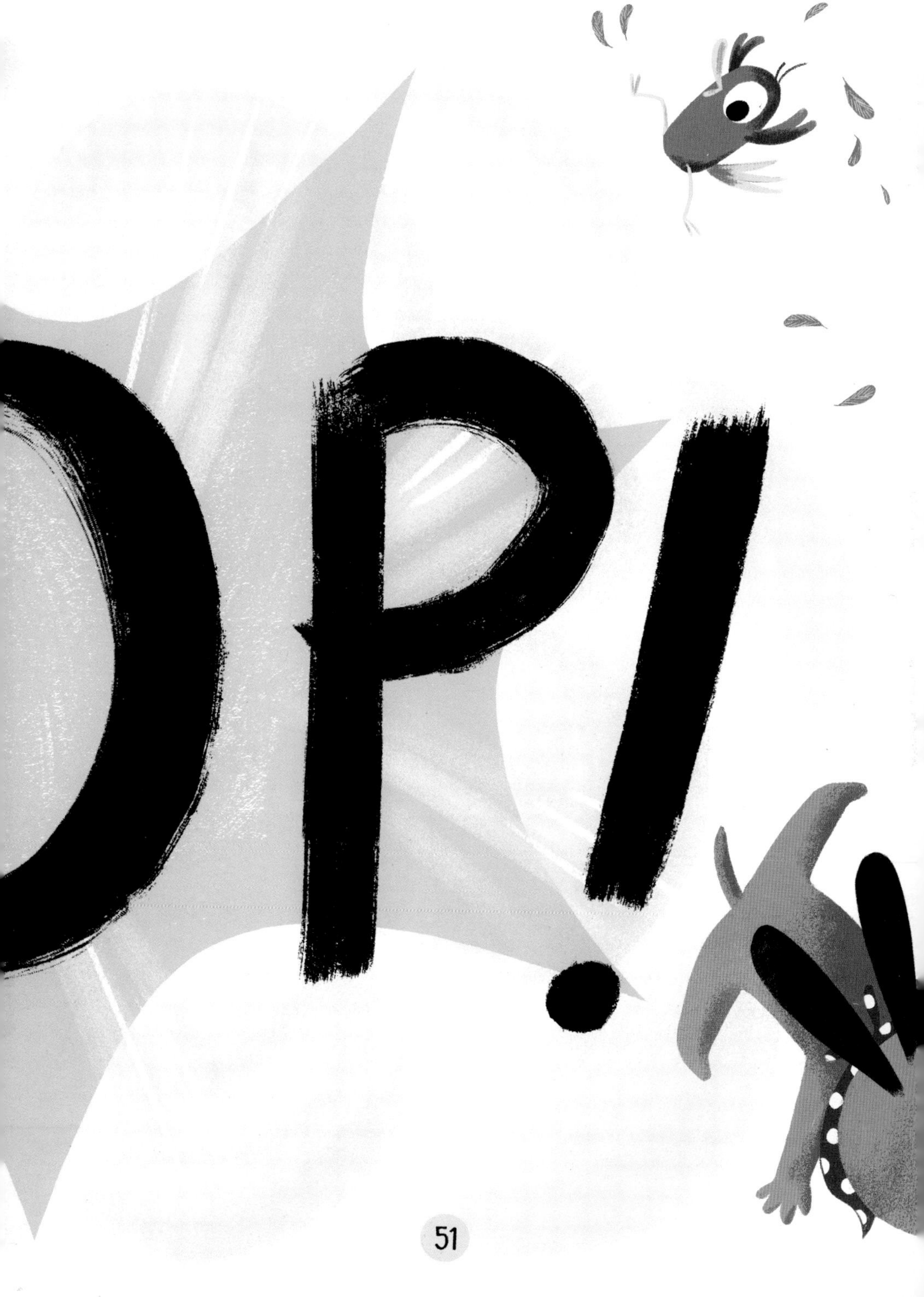
OP!

You did it, Pup-Pup. You popped the bubble!

Yeah. I did!

You saved me!!!

hug hug

Yes, and popping the bubble was FUN!

I'm NEVER popping bubbles again.

Well, I'm NEVER blowing bubbles again.

WHEW!

53

But we still love bubbles, don't we?

Yes, we do love bubbles!

54

bubble soap mix

SUPER BUBBLE MIX

55

Chapter 6
We Still Love Bubbles!

I love BLOWING bubbles!

bubbl soap

POP

POP

POP

POP

POP

♥ I love POPPING bubbles!

57

Hungry for another Bobo and Pup-Pup book?

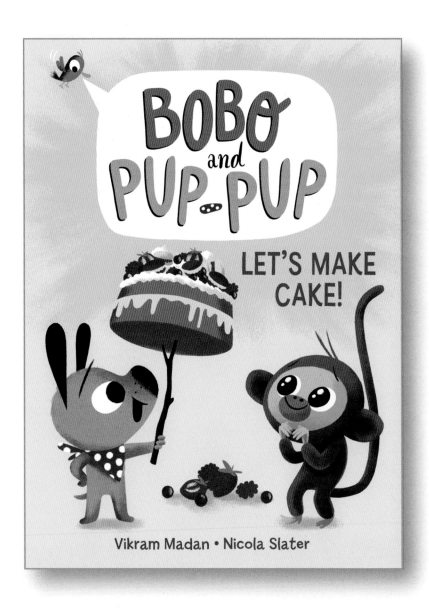

BOBO and PUP-PUP

LET'S MAKE CAKE!

Vikram Madan • Nicola Slater

Vikram Madan grew up in India, where he really wanted to be a cartoonist but ended up an engineer. After many years in the tech industry, he finally came to his senses and followed his heart back to humor. He lives near Seattle, where—in addition to making whimsical and humorous visual art—he writes and illustrates books of funny poems, including the *Kirkus Reviews* Best Book *A Hatful of Dragons* and the Moonbeam Award Winners *The Bubble Collector* and *Lord of the Bubbles*. Visit him at VikramMadan.com.

Nicola Slater lives with her family in the wild and windy north of England. She has illustrated many middle-grade novels and picture books, including *Where Is My Pink Sweater?* (which she also wrote), *Leaping Lemmings!, A Skunk in My Bunk!*, and Margaret Wise Brown's *Manners*, a Little Golden Book. In her spare time she likes looking at animals, camping in the rain, and tickling her children. You can follow her on Twitter at @nicolaslater.